The Thorn Thicket

Jibber Jabber

ACKNOWLEDGEMENTS

In an extraordinary kingdom, lived two ordinary brothers named Percy and Albert. Percy and Albert were bakers who made the best cakes, breads, and pastries in all the land. Like nearly everyone else in the kingdom, the brothers were poor though they worked hard.

One day, the king decided he would have a big party. This was not unusual. The king had a party almost every week. He celebrated everything. This time, the king was having a party because his cousin's sister's daughter's great aunt's cat recently had kittens. This was indeed cause for celebration. As usual, the king ordered the two brothers to bake him a humongous cake. They only had one day to make the cake, so the brothers stayed up all night. After many hours of baking, frosting, and decorating, they delivered the largest and most beautiful cake they had ever made. The cake was shaped like a giant orange cat, and the inside tasted like chocolate, vanilla, and cookies and cream.

In spite of their magnificent work, the brothers did not expect to be paid well. The selfish king never gave them much money. However, the bakers were astonished when they were told they would not be paid at all! Percy, the older brother, walked away, disappointed and worried. He wondered how they would be able to afford their food and supplies. Albert, the younger brother, did not walk away. He threw off his cloak and stood in the middle of the crowded ballroom.

"We will not leave until we are paid a just price," Albert boldly declared.

The king's face paled only for a moment, then turned crimson with rage.

"How dare you interrupt my celebration, peasant!" the king screeched. "You are a lowly baker! You were given the privilege, the honor, of baking a cake for your king, and now you want money?"

The furious king seized his sword. The prince, who was far kinder and more reasonable than his father, tried to intercede, but it was no use. The king lifted his sword and chopped off poor Albert's head, leaving Percy to carry the remains of his brother home.

Fortunately, even though Albert's head was chopped off, he wasn't dead. You see, people were a lot hardier back in the day. They were much more difficult to kill. Albert wasn't dead, but he soon would be if Percy did nothing to help him. Percy needed magic to re-attach the head. There was only one thing that would work: he needed two magical blue rose petals.

They were very easy to find. Percy knew exactly where they were. Everyone did. If you walked over the hill, across the rickety bridge, into the deep dark of the forest in the deep dark of the night, found the tree with the magic door, walked through the magic door which served as a magic portal, climbed over the mountain of death and gloom, and went into the enchanted thorn thicket, you would find the blue roses. It wasn't that complicated. So, that's what Percy did.

He walked over the hill, across the rickety bridge, into the deep dark of the forest in the deep dark of the night, found the tree with the magic door, walked through the magic door which served as a magic portal, and climbed over the mountain of death and gloom.

But that was the easy part. The hard part was getting through the thorn thicket. The thicket was quite temperamental. It didn't like visitors. As soon as the baker stepped into the thicket, it struck him with its thorns. The baker stood completely still as the thicket continued to attack and prick him. He did not swat the branches away or even try to protect himself. He did not move at all.

At last, when the thicket saw that Percy had no intention of causing harm, it stopped attacking him. It parted its branches and allowed the badly injured baker to walk through. There, in the middle of the thicket, were the most beautiful blue roses.

"You must only take what is needed, or else I will never let you go," the thicket warned him.

The baker nodded, plucking two blue petals and putting them in his pocket. He walked out of the thorn thicket, climbed over the mountain of death and gloom, walked through the magic door in the tree which served as a magic portal, through the deep dark of the forest in the deep dark of the night, across the rickety bridge, over the hill, and returned to his home.

He put his brother's body on the table and assembled him as best he could. Reaching into his pocket, Percy withdrew the two blue petals and placed them over his brother's eyes. The petals immediately shriveled up. Albert opened his eyes and sat up with his head once again attached! The brothers were overjoyed. There was a brief moment of panic when they thought they had put the head on the wrong way, but they soon realized that it was only his cloak that was on backwards. They were happy. Their neighbors were happy. Everyone was happy . . . well, except the king.

When the king heard the news, he screamed and stomped his feet. In his fit of rage, he had chopped off someone's head only for it to be completely re-attached the next day. How dare they reverse his wrathful misdeed! The malicious king wanted to punish the brothers, so he devised a sneaky, underhanded, devious scheme. It's so awful, I don't even know if I should tell you.

But I will. The king used a bag of poisoned flour. It wasn't creative, but that didn't matter as long as it was effective, and it was very effective. Late that night, the king sneaked into the baker's home and switched out a bag of ordinary flour with his poisoned one. The next day, the bakers used the flour to make bread. Percy liked to lick any extra batter off the spoon. As soon as he tasted it, he collapsed to the floor.

Don't worry. He wasn't dead. I told you, people back then were tough. Percy wasn't dead, but Albert couldn't wake him up. Percy snored loudly, sound asleep. Albert knew there were only two ways to wake him. One was true love's kiss. Unfortunately, Percy and his girlfriend had gotten into a big argument the week before. They weren't broken up, but they weren't exactly together either. Let's just say they weren't in a good place. She couldn't kiss him. It would have been too awkward and a bit presumptuous.

There was only one other way to save Percy: Albert had to get the magical blue rose petals. He grabbed his sword and began his journey. He walked over the hill, across the rickety bridge, into - well, you are by now familiar with the overcomplicated journey, so let's just skip ahead to when he reached the thorn thicket.

As soon as Albert stepped into the thicket, it pricked him harshly, but he struck back with his sword. On and on they fought. At last, the thicket realized that Albert would never give up, so it relented. It parted its branches and allowed the wounded baker to walk through. There, in the middle of the thicket, he found the most beautiful blue roses.

The thicket warned him, "You must only take what is needed, or else I will never let you go."

The baker plucked two blue petals and put them in his pocket. He walked out of the thorn thicket and made the convoluted journey home.

After he placed the petals over his brother's eyes, the petals shriveled up. Percy opened his eyes and was immediately well again. They were so happy. The neighbors were so happy, but I bet you can guess who wasn't happy. The king. He had tried to kill two kind, courageous people, and yet they somehow managed to live. I can't imagine anything more frustrating for him.

So, he decided he needed to destroy those blue roses. What was the point of killing people if their loved ones could use those pesky flowers to save them? The king trudged over the hill, stumbled his way across the rickety bridge, wandered in the deep dark of the forest in the deep dark of the night, barely found the tree with the magic door, tripped through the magic door which served as a magic portal, and panted over the mountain of death and gloom.

He approached the enchanted thorn thicket. The moody thicket was even more irritated than usual due to its last encounter with the aggressive baker. It did not want to let the king through, so the king raised his sword, charged into the thicket, and began to fight. The king, however, did not have the same determination and courage as the bakers did. He soon gave up and tried to escape, but the thicket would not let him go. It continued pricking him, and the king was never able to leave.

After some time, when everyone assumed the king would never come back, the prince was crowned king. After his coronation, there was a party. The new king asked the two bakers to make him a delicious cake. But this time, the bakers were paid well and no one had their head chopped off.

The End.

Thank you for reading my book! Here's a free postcard you can download here:

https://jibberjabberblog.blogspot.com/2023/05/the-thorn-thicket-postcard.html

You can get free coloring pages here!

https://jibberjabberblog.blogspot.com/2023/05/free-thorn-thicket-coloring-pages.html

 Book narration available here!

https://jibberjabberblog.blogspot.com/2023/05/the-thorn-thicket-video.html

9 781948 921114